My Gran's Different

For my grandmothers: Goog, who I never knew, and Gran, whose courage and strength were amazing. S.L.

With thanks to all who helped with this book. C.M.

My Gran's Different

Sue Lawson & Caroline Magerl

Simply Read Books

Published in 2005 by Simply Read Books
www.simplyreadbooks.com

Text copyright © Sue Lawson 2003, 2005
Illustrations copyright © Caroline Magerl 2003

First published by Thomas C. Lothian Pty. Ltd.

Cataloguing in Publication Data

Lawson, Sue, 1969-
  My Gran's different / Sue Lawson ; Illustrated by Caroline Magerl

ISBN 1-894965-16-7

  I. Magerl, Caroline II. Title

PZ7.L39My 2005   j823'.92   C2005-900576-9

10 9 8 7 6 5 4 3 2 1

Designed by Mark Davis
Prepress by Print+Publish, Port Melbourne
Printed in China by SNP Leefung

Sophie's nanna bakes sponge cakes as high as my school bag and fills them with shiny strawberries and clouds of whipped cream.

But my gran's different.

Michael's grandma wears lipstick as bright as a clown's nose and leaves big smudges on his cheeks when she kisses him.

But my gran's different.

Jonty's granny catches the train to the game every week. She wears a black and white hat and screams at the referees.

But my gran's different.

Raffie's nonna drives a florist van. She delivers roses, daffodils and irises all over the city.

But my gran's different.

Claire's oma used to live in Holland. She wears wooden shoes called clogs when she works in her garden.

But my gran's different.

Alex's grandmother knits all weekend. She makes Alex scarves as long as skipping ropes, and sweaters that scritch and scratch his neck.

But my gran's different.

Rosie's Gramma Joan and Uncle Pat are touring the States in an RV.
They send her postcards from every town they visit.

But my gran's different.

Mitchell's nanny owns an art gallery on Main Street and teaches people about dot paintings.

But my gran's different.

Dimitri's baba died before he was born, but he has a photo of her in his bedroom.

My gran's not dead, but she is different.

My gran stares out the window and rocks in time with the breeze.

Because my gran is different.

She can't remember who she is.

But that's all right, because I remember who she is.